CRISPY

in

THE BIRTHDAY BAND

By Justine Korman
Illustrated by Dean Yeagle
Painted by Mike Favata

Every year Tim looked forward to his birthday,
but it seemed like something always went wrong.
One year he got the measles and gave it to
everyone.

The year after that, the basement flooded and spoiled his party.

Another year Tim was supposed to go to an amusement park with his friends, but it rained the whole day.

"This year will be different," Tim's parents promised.

Tim sure hoped it would be. He peeked in drawers and listened at doorways, hoping to get some clue about a birthday celebration. He thought he might even find the new harmonica he was hoping for. But he didn't find a trace of party plans or presents.

When the big day finally came, Tim jumped out of bed and ran downstairs.

His parents and his sister, Karen, were already
having breakfast.

"Good morning," they said, as if it were any other
day.

Nobody shouted "Happy birthday!" or started to
sing.

"They've forgotten," thought Tim sadly as he ate his breakfast.

Soon Tim's family rushed off to their Saturday chores and left him alone at the table.

Tim sat by himself in the quiet kitchen, and a big lonely tear rolled down his cheek. Then he heard a strange sound.

"What was that?" Tim wondered, and he held his breath and listened. It was music, but it wasn't coming from the radio.

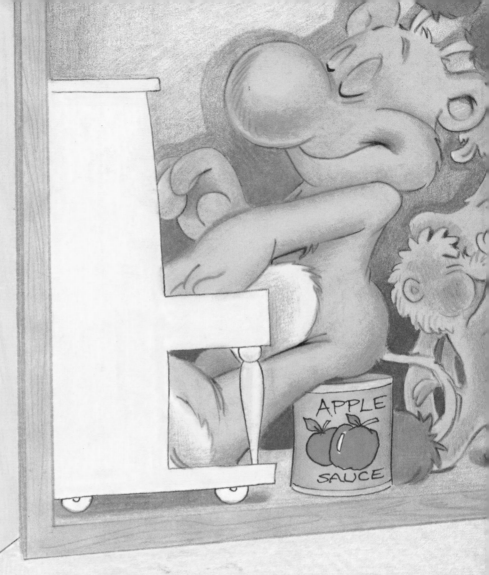

Tim followed the sound to the cabinet, where he
saw the most amazing thing—a band of tiny
animals playing happy music.

Tim rubbed his eyes and blinked, but the animals
were still there, proudly playing their instruments.

At the end of the song the funny little piano
player exclaimed, "Ah-cha-cha-cha."

"Who...what?" Tim stammered.
"An audience!" Crispy declared happily.
"My name's Tim," Tim managed to say.

"Let me introduce myself. I'm Crispy, and this is the Crispy Critters® cereal band," said the piano player.

Then all at once the other animals played a chord on their instruments and took a little bow.

"I've never heard of an animal band before," said
Tim.

"Neither had we, but, indubitably, here we are,"
said Crispy. "And we've made up a song about it."

Tim listened with astonishment as the band started to play.

"Most sheep like to bleat, but I like to keep the beat," sang Sam the Ram with a roll on his drums.

"Lions always roar, but I like singing more," Brian the Lion sang.

Then Camille the Camel and Dewey the Donkey sang a duet. "We'd rather play than bray!"

And Zippo the Hippo sang, "I like the piccolo because it sounds so mellow. It sounds so different from the hippo's loud bellow."

The animals stopped suddenly in the middle of
their song.

"What's the matter?" asked Crispy. "Don't you
like our sound?"

"You're really great," Tim replied. But he didn't
sound very excited.

"Is something wrong?" Crispy asked gently. "I've got two furry ears just made for listening."

Tim explained what seemed to happen on his birthday each year. He added gloomily, "But this year is the worst. No one's remembered my birthday at all."

With that, Crispy struck a note on his piano, and the other animals quickly joined him in a joyous version of "Happy Birthday to You."

"Hey, wait for me!" said Tim, pulling his old harmonica out of his pocket. It wasn't the big new one he had hoped for, but the sound was still quite nice.

All morning Tim and his new friends played music together. They were having such a good time that Tim forgot all about his birthday until his mother called from downstairs.

"Tim! Come down to the basement, please. I need help folding the laundry."

"Chores on my birthday!" Tim muttered crossly.
He went sadly to the basement.

"Mom?" Tim called into the darkness from the top of the stairs.

Then he clicked on the light switch and...
"Surprise!"
All of Tim's friends and relatives were there in the basement, which was covered with bright paper streamers and filled with balloons and presents. There was even a big cake with candles!

Tim's father handed him a brightly wrapped package.

"Open it," he urged. "Did you think we'd forgotten?"

Tim tore the paper, and inside the box he found a shiny new harmonica that made beautiful sounds.

Tim couldn't wait to play a tune on it, so he started with one of the songs he'd been practicing with the animal band.

Before he finished the song, the Crispy Critters®
cereal band joined him. They played all afternoon,
and everyone danced, clapped, and tapped their feet
to the music.

"Ah-cha-cha-cha!" exclaimed Crispy. "Indubitably,
we are a hit!"

"Indub…indububblebees…" Tim stammered.
"Indubitably," Crispy corrected.
Tim declared, "This is the best birthday anyone ever had!"